SALMON BOY

A LEGEND OF THE SECHELT PEOPLE

Nightwood Editions acknowledges the financial support of the Canada Council for the Arts and the Province of British Columbia through the British Columbia Arts Council, for its publishing activities.

THE CANADA COUNCIL | LE CONSEIL DES ARTS
FOR THE ARTS | DU CANADA
SINCE 1957 | DEPUIS 1957

Nightwood Editions,
RR5 S26 C13, Gibsons, BC Canada V0N 1V0

Distributed by Harbour Publishing.

Printed in Canada
Design by Roger Handling, Terra Firma Digital Arts.
Additional illustrations by Kim LaFave.

Canadian Cataloguing in Publication Data

Joe, Donna, 1948-
  Salmon boy

  ISBN 0-88971-166-6

  1. Sechelt Indians—Folklore. 2. Salmon—Folklore. 3. Legends—British Columbia. I. Craigan, Charlie. II. Title.
E99.S218J65 1998   j398.24'52756   C99-910009-2

SALMON BOY

A LEGEND OF THE SECHELT PEOPLE

BY DONNA JOE
ILLUSTRATED BY CHARLIE CRAIGAN

NIGHTWOOD EDITIONS

Long, long ago, a boy lived in a village called k̲alpilin, the winter home of the Sechelt Nation. The boy's people lived in great longhouses along the seashore. It was a good place to live but the people often went hungry during the long winter months. In those days so long ago the salmon did not fill the creeks and rivers of Sechelt.

One beautiful summer day, the boy decided to escape the heat by going for a swim in the sea beside k̲alpilin. As he swam out from the shore, a giant chum salmon seized him and pulled him down under the sea to the country of the salmon people.

Although the country of the salmon people was beneath the sea, it was dry and the salmon people walked about the same as people do above the sea. Everyone lived in cedar plank houses and all along the beach their canoes were lined up in a row.

The giant chum salmon took the boy to his home and made him a slave. The boy was fascinated by these very special people and took careful note of everything they did.

Some women made cedar root baskets and hats. Others made shredded cedar bark capes, skirts and mats. Some men carved house poles, welcome poles, feast bowls and dugout canoes from the wood of the cedar.

In the winter, when the work of the summer was done and the longhouses were full of the salmon they had dried and smoked, they celebrated with singing and dancing for weeks at a time. Each house had its own singers and dancers. This was also the time for storytelling. Their food in winter months was salmon which had been smoked and dried the summer before.

In the spring, the people were hungry for food that was fresh. First they gathered the eggs or roe of the herring, then they peeled and ate the soft green shoots of the salmonberry and thimbleberry bushes. Soon berries ripened on the bushes and the people ate their fill of the tasty fruit.

In the summer, families left their winter longhouses, packed their things into their dugout canoes and paddled across the water to small cedar sheds where they lived and worked during the sunny weather. During this time, the people picked large amounts of salal berries, huckleberries, blueberries and blackberries, and dried them on mats for use in the winter. They also fished the spring, pink and sockeye salmon. In the fall the chum and coho started up stream to spawn. Great quantities of these fish were dried, smoked and stored away to feed the people during the winter.

The boy studied the salmon people for one year, memorizing all the things they did to keep from going hungry. In the fall, the salmon people got ready to start upstream to their spawning grounds. All the little salmon began to cry, saying they wanted to go, too. The elders told them they could not go until they were four years old, but the boy was allowed to go with the giant chum salmon who had captured him.

When they were ready to start, they took all their canoes and paddled to a small stream. They were a glad and merry party, and sang as they jumped in the water.

When the salmon went up stream into shallow water, the little boy jumped out, went home to <u>k</u>alpilin and told the Sechelt people about the many wonderful things he had seen in the land of the salmon people.

In this way the Sechelt people learned many things. The most important thing they learned was that the salmon are themselves a proud race. They are happy to come ashore each year and give their rich flesh to feed the people of the land, but they must be treated with respect. The people were on no account to break the neck of fish caught in the early days of the run or the salmon would never return. The salmon creeks and rivers must always be kept clean and healthy, and each family must take only as many fish as it needed, never wasting any.

From that time forward, the Sechelt Nation always treated the salmon properly and its people never went hungry.

ABOUT CHARLIE CRAIGAN

Charles Joseph (Charlie) Craigan, who illustrated this story, was born in Sechelt BC in 1969. His natural artistic talent began showing itself while he was still a Grade 5 student at Sechelt Elementary and was further developed while working with carvers Arnold Jones and Jamie Jeffries. Charlie is a member of the Sechelt Indian Band and lives on the band lands in Sechelt.

Charlie dedicates the illustrations in this book to the elders of the Sechelt nation.

ABOUT DONNA JOE

Donna Joe, who retold this story, was born a member of the Sechelt Indian Band on the beautiful Sunshine Coast of British Columbia. As a child she used to go gillnet fishing with her mom and dad, Marjorie and Cyprian August. In 1953 she began attending residential school and went on to complete a Bachelor of Education at the University of British Columbia (NITEP), where she continues in a master's program. She works for the Sechelt School District and Sechelt Indian Band as Supervisor of shashishalhem (Sechelt language). Donna and her husband Vern have three grown children and five grandchildren.